DISNEY's
My Very First Winnie the Pooh™

Don't Be Scared, Piglet and Roo!

Adapted by
Barbara Gaines Winkelman

Illustrated by
Kim Raymond

SCHOLASTIC INC.

New York Toronto London Auckland Sydney
Mexico City New Delhi Hong Kong Buenos Aires

Special thanks to Paul Windle (inking) and Paul Hogg (background painting)

Published by Scholastic Inc., 90 Old Sherman Turnpike, Danbury, CT 06816
by arrangement with Disney Licensed Publishing.

SCHOLASTIC and associated logos are trademarks
and/or registered trademarks of Scholastic Inc.

ISBN 0-7172-8923-0

Printed in the U.S.A.

One night, strange sounds woke Piglet from a deep sleep.

Whoosh. Rat-a-tat-tat. Rat-a-tat-tat. Whoosh. Rat-a-tat-tat. Rat-a-tat-tat.

"What was that?" Piglet called, sitting straight up in his bed. He was afraid of what he might see. Using all his courage, Piglet looked around. Suddenly he saw dark, scary shapes! There was a dark night creature in his room!

"Oh, Pooh, could it have been a heffalump?" Piglet asked his friend the next day. "It was very scary-looking, and it made a lot of noise. I couldn't sleep all night."

"Perhaps you should go see if it's still there," said Pooh. "You might be able to tell better in daylight."

"Come with me, Pooh?" begged Piglet. "My house seems scary now, even in daylight."

"Of course I will, Piglet," answered Pooh.

"What did the scary shapes look like?" Pooh whispered as they entered Piglet's house.

Piglet hid his eyes. "I'm n-not sure. They were dark and squiggled along the wall. I thought it was a heffalump so I went under the covers."

They tiptoed into the bedroom. Nothing happened. "What exactly did you hear, Piglet, and where did it come from?" asked Pooh.

"I heard *Whoosh. Rat-a-tat-tat. Rat-a-tat-tat. Whoosh. Rat-a-tat-tat. Rat-a-tat-tat*, and it came from there," said Piglet, pointing toward the window over his bed.

Pooh crossed to the window. Suddenly there were strange sounds. *Whoosh. Rat-a-tat-tat. Rat-a-tat-tat. Whoosh. Rat-a-tat-tat. Rat-a-tat-tat.*

Pooh opened the window and the sounds grew louder. Piglet scrambled under the bed.

"Oh, my," remarked Pooh, "listen to that wind! It is so strong, it's bending the tree branches over far enough to knock on your windows. Oh, bother! I hope the wind doesn't blow the old bee tree down!"

 P iglet peered out from under the bed.

"W-wind?" he said.

Pooh and Piglet looked at each other.

"*The wind!*" Piglet suddenly shouted. "Of course, Pooh! It was the *wind!*"

"That was the *whoosh*?" asked Pooh. "The wind was blowing through the trees?"

"Yes!" cried Piglet. "I should have known! And the *rat-a-tat-tat* sound is the tree branches knocking at the window. Oh, Pooh, that's not scary at all!"

"But what about the creature I *saw*?" Piglet asked later, while they were having a smackerel. "What if *it* was a heffalump and *it* comes back?"

"Keep a night-light on, perhaps?" said Pooh.

"I *did* have a night-light on, but it didn't help!" squeaked Piglet. "When I sat up, there were dark shapes . . . on the *o-other side* o-of the bed . . . . Hah!" Pooh and Piglet looked at each other.

"I may be a bear of little brain," Pooh said, "but it sounds to me like a shadow . . . ."

"My shadow!" cried Piglet. "Of course!"

Piglet slept soundly that night. The dark shapes and *whoosh, rat-a-tat-tat* sounds didn't worry him anymore, because now he knew what they were.

Next day, Piglet told the story to his friends.

"I couldn't sleep because I heard strange sounds and saw scary shapes the other night."

"What sounds?" Roo wanted to know.

"Oogly-boogly *grrrowwly*, sounds, right?" interrupted Tigger.

But Piglet shook his head. "No, they went *Whoosh. Rat-a-tat-tat. Rat-a-tat-tat. Whoosh. Rat-a-tat-tat. Rat-a-tat-tat.*"

"What were the scary shapes?" asked Roo.

"They were dark and squiggly," answered Piglet. "I thought it was a heffalump!"

"Downright frightening," nodded Eeyore.

"Come along, Roo, dear," said Kanga. "We are meeting Christopher Robin now." Kanga scooped Roo into her pouch and hopped away. Piglet noticed Roo's eyes were very wide.

"Oh, d-d-dear!" Piglet said. "Roo's scared. He didn't hear the end of my story. The strange sounds and scary shapes turned out to be just wind and shadows!"

That night, Kanga put Roo to bed just as always. They read a book. Then Kanga tucked Roo in, patted him, and gave him a kiss.

"I love you, dear," said Kanga. She blew out the candle and went out of the room.

Roo was all alone.

Whoosh. Rat-a-tat-tat. Rat-a-tat-tat. Whoosh. Rat-a-tat-tat. Rat-a-tat-tat.

There were the strange sounds Piglet had told him about!

"Could Piglet's heffalump be *here*?" Roo wondered. He sat up and peeked. Sure enough, there were dark, scary shapes in his room!

The strange sounds got louder and louder. *WHOOSH. RAT-A-TAT-TAT. RAT-A-TAT-TAT. WHOOSH. RAT-A-TAT-TAT. RAT-A-TAT-TAT.*

More and more dark, scary night creatures squiggled around the room. Roo could not sleep. He was very frightened!

"Mama! Come back!" Roo called out. "I'm scared! *Mama!*"

In an instant, Kanga was in Roo's room.

"What's wrong, dear?" she asked gently.

"There are strange sounds and scary shapes!" whimpered Roo, using Piglet's words.

"Show me," said Kanga. "Where are the scary shapes?"

Roo pointed to the walls.

"Oh, yes," said Kanga. "Those are shadows Roo, dear! They are from the moon shining through the tree branches outside. Shadows can be fun! When we know what they are, we can pretend they're something *not* scary, but nice. Let's pretend they are the arms of friends, reaching out to hug us."

"Or . . . or beautiful plants growing on the walls?" asked Roo.

"That's right, dear!" Kanga smiled.

"Now, let's listen for the strange sounds."

They were silent for a moment.

Whoosh. Rat-a-tat-tat. Rat-a-tat-tat. Whoosh. Rat-a-tat-tat. Rat-a-tat-tat.

"Come over to the window with me, Roo, dear," said Kanga. "See the branches moving? Those noises are from the wind knocking the branches against the window. They make a nice rhythm. Maybe we can make up a lullaby to sing along with the sounds."

So Kanga sang this lullaby to Roo:

Now it's time to sleep, my dear
And wake up fresh tomorrow.
When you listen you will hear
The woods outside your window.
When you look around, you'll see
Their shadows dancing about you.

And when Kanga had finished
singing, Roo was fast asleep.

Next morning, Roo was just starting his breakfast when Piglet arrived, all out of breath.

"Roo! I wanted to tell you—"

"It *wasn't* heffalumps, Piglet!" Roo interrupted.

"Yes!" Piglet gasped. "How did you know?"

"Because they came here!" cried Roo. "But Mama showed me it was *shadows* and *wind* and branches knocking on the window."

"And we won't be scared in the night *anymore*!" said Piglet.